FANNY'S DREAM

Caralyn Buehner ✳ *Pictures by* Mark Buehner

Dial Books for Young Readers ✳ New York

Published by Dial Books for Young Readers
A Division of Penguin Books USA Inc.
375 Hudson Street
New York, New York 10014

Designed by Nancy R. Leo
Printed in Hong Kong
First Edition
3 5 7 9 10 8 6 4

Library of Congress Cataloging in Publication Data
Buehner, Caralyn.
Fanny's dream / by Caralyn Buehner; pictures by Mark Buehner.
p. cm.
Summary: Fanny Agnes is a sturdy farm girl who dreams of marrying a prince,
but when her fairy godmother doesn't show up, she decides on a local farmer instead.
ISBN 0-8037-1496-3 (trade).—ISBN 0-8037-1497-1 (library)
[1. Marriage—Fiction. 2. Farm life—Fiction.]
I. Buehner, Mark, ill. II. Title.
PZ7.B884Fan 1996 [E]—dc20 94-31910 CIP AC

The art for this book was prepared by using oil paints over acrylics.

* * *

In memory of Winnie and Leland Harris,
who lived the law of the harvest

ONCE UPON A TIME in a wild Wyoming town there lived a sturdy girl named Fanny Agnes. She worked from sunup to sundown on her daddy's farm, but she had her dreams.

She was going to marry a prince.

Or at least the mayor's son. He would be tall, handsome, and have a *dozen* carriages. He would kiss her hand, dress her in silks and satins, and never let her do another stitch of work. If it could happen once upon a time, Fanny believed, it could happen again. After all, what were fairy godmothers for?

When she heard that the mayor was going to give a grand ball, Fanny was so excited she pulled up a row of carrots and left the weeds instead. This had to be it!

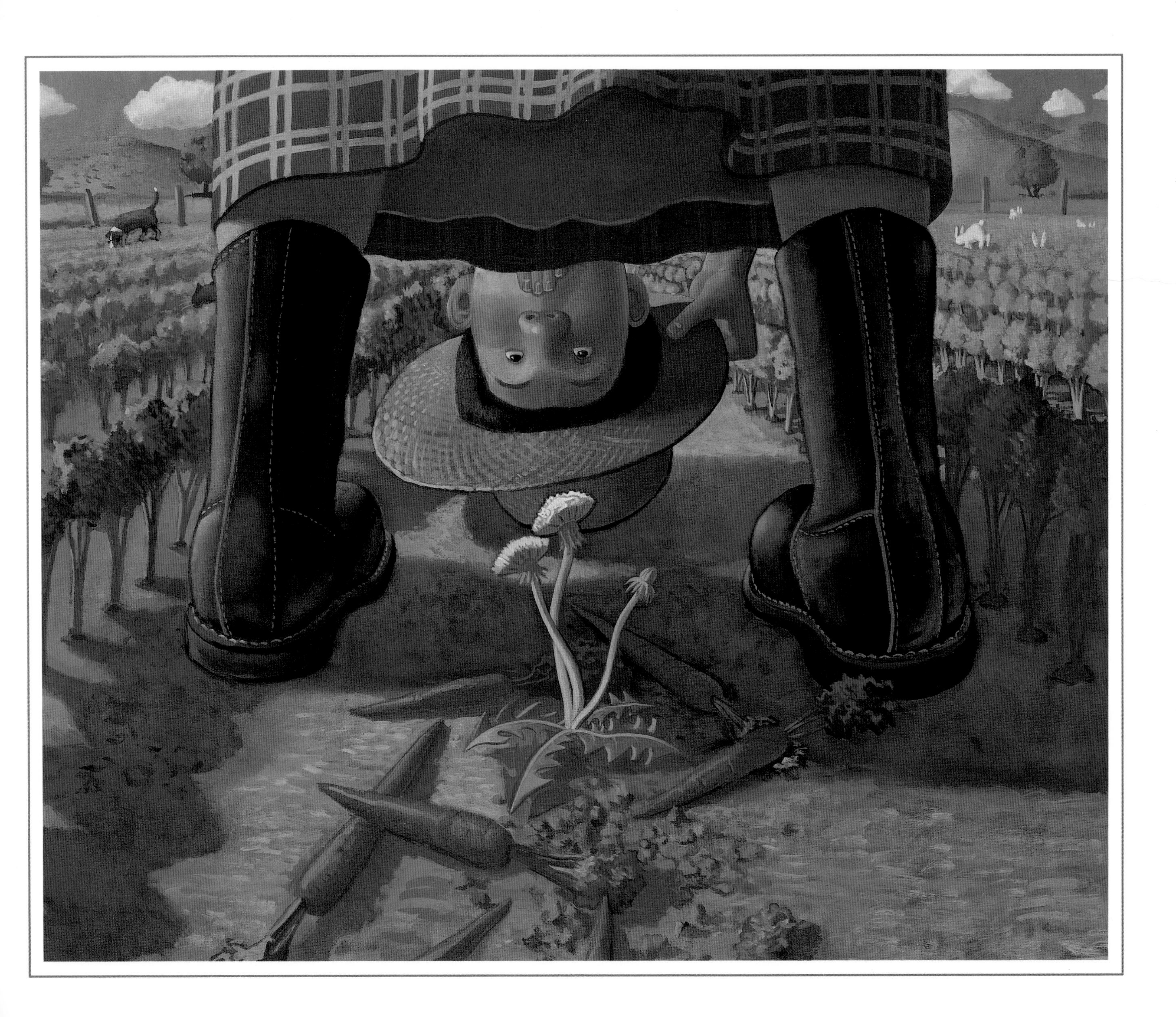

Fanny couldn't resist telling her girlfriends at the hat shop.

"I'm going to the ball, and I'm going to marry a prince. Or someone like that."

"You?" the girls hooted. "You're not beautiful, you have nothing to wear, and you're about as graceful as an elephant!"

But Fanny didn't mind. She knew her dreams would come true.

Fanny told her brother at dinner that she was going to the ball.

"You?" he roared with laughter. "You're as big as an ox!" When Fanny got to the part about the fairy godmother, her brother was rolling on the floor.

"I read about a girl in a book," Fanny said defensively, "and I know just what to do."

That night Fanny dressed in her best calico and went out into the garden to wait for her fairy godmother. She waited for a long time. After awhile she pulled up some weeds. She could see the mayor's mansion across the valley, all lit up. She could almost hear the music. When it got too dark to pull weeds, she washed her hands and sat down. The moon came out, big and full.

"Hey, Fanny!" a voice called. Fanny jumped up to meet her fairy godmother.

But it wasn't her fairy godmother, only Heber Jensen. Heber was cheerful and pleasant, and had always liked Fanny, but heavens, he was so short! Fanny almost started crying.

"What are you doing out here so late, Fanny?" Heber asked.

"I'm waiting for my fairy godmother," sniffled Fanny. "I wanted to go to the ball."

Heber thought this over.

"Can you twirl and waltz and curtsy?" asked Heber.

"No," said Fanny. Then she said, "But I know how to harness a horse, plow a field, and shuck corn."

"Well, then," Heber said, "do you know how to use twenty forks and spoons, drink from a goblet, and eat snails?"

Fanny wrinkled her nose. "No, but I can cure a ham, kill and dress a chicken, milk ten cows, and make bread."

"Well," Heber teased, "can you simper and flutter your fan and cinch up your waist?"

"No," Fanny giggled, "but I can spread manure!"

"We-ell-ll, Fanny," said Heber slowly, "I'm not a prince and I don't live in a castle. But I have one hundred and sixty acres, a little log house, and dreams of my own. I need a wife who will work by my side, through thick and thin, sweat and joy, and be glad for good food and great company. Will you, Fanny?"

Even with all that moonlight it took Fanny an hour to give up her dreams. She shook Heber awake.

"I don't do windows."

"Okay," said Heber.

So Fanny married Heber. She helped him plow the north field. She planted potatoes in the garden and pansies in the front. She thinned the beets, fed the chickens, threshed the beans. She held the sheep while Heber sheared them, churned butter, and slopped the pigs.

In the winter Fanny would bring the washing in, frozen stiff, and hang it in the house to thaw. In the evenings Heber would crack nuts and tell stories while Fanny did the mending.

Sometimes, when she needed a good laugh, Fanny would stitch the flaps shut on Heber's long johns, then wait to hear him hollering from the outhouse.

As for Heber, he figured that it hadn't been easy for Fanny to give up her dreams, so he made it a point to wait on her at least once a day, as if she *were* a princess, and every so often he wiped the grime off the windows.

The next year the twins were born. Fanny washed diapers and hung them on the stove, washed diapers and hung them across the mantel, washed diapers and hung them from the doorknobs. Heber rocked David and Ethan.

When the twins were five, Davy stuck his socks in the toaster and burned the house down. Fanny grabbed the new baby and the twins before the roof caved in. Heber ran from the fields to see his dreams smoking.

Then Fanny and Heber built the house again.

One night Fanny went out into the garden to pick a melon. The moon was full, the air was soft.

Fanny sat down and looked up at the stars in the night sky. Then she looked across the valley at the mayor's house, which was all lit up. She could almost hear the music.

"Sorry I'm late!" a voice sang out.

Fanny Agnes jumped up as her fairy godmother twinkled down.

"You poor dear, having to wait all these years," her fairy godmother gushed. "But there's still time! There's a visiting colonel at the mayor's ball tonight. Just leave it to me! I'll fix everything!"

"But..." Fanny hesitated.

"What's the matter?" Her fairy godmother stamped impatiently. "Do you want to go to the ball or not?"

Fanny looked down at her work-roughened hands. She looked at the little house where Heber was reading to Davy, Ethan, and Edna Faye.

"Not," Fanny said, and she went back into the house.

"Who were you talking to out there, Fan?" Heber asked.

"My fairy godmother, Hebie."

Heber laughed. "Oh, sure! And I'm the Prince of Sahiba."

"Close enough," Fanny winked, "close enough."

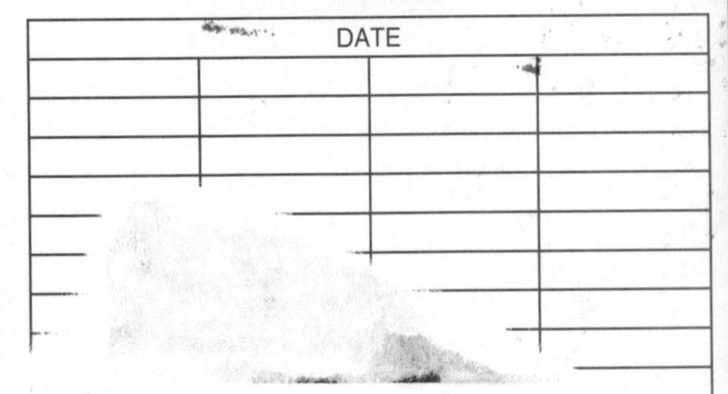